Once there was a frog named Alice who lived in a little pond. Alice knew every inch of the pond's murky bottom and every hiding place among the reeds. She knew too, that she could swim from one side to the other with twenty-eight kicks of her back legs.

Guy Billout

THE FROG WHO WANTED TO SEE THE SEA

Creative Editions

On warm afternoons, dragonflies appeared out of nowhere and settled on the cattails at the edge of the pond. They peered at Alice with their big mirror eyes before zipping away. Alice watched them and  wondered where they went. In the winter, Alice saw seagulls circling high above her pond. She loved watching them wheel, but they always vanished as spring approached. Alice wondered why.

4

One morning, feeling strangely courageous, the little frog asked a seagull about the world beyond the cattails.

This curious frog amused the bird, who patiently described all that he had seen—the towering mountains, the big gray cities, and the airplanes in the clouds. He finished by telling her of the sea—how he flew there in the spring for food, and how one could not see the other side it was so big.

"So it is bigger than the pond?" asked Alice, her eyes wide.

"Much bigger," said the seagull.

Alice tried to picture such a large pond. She wondered how many kicks it would take to swim from one side to the other. Then, one morning, the gulls were gone. It was spring.

Several days later, Alice made up her mind: she was going to see the sea.

The seagull had explained to Alice how he followed the river to the sea.

Carrying a rolled-up lily pad, she set off through woods and fields, stopping only to hide when she heard a prowling owl or fox. At dawn, she reached the river.

Alice had never seen so much water and was frightened by its movement.

Summoning all her courage, she hopped into the rapid current, using her lily pad as a raft.

Alice enjoyed the ride. She was happy to see some familiar faces later in the day. A pair of dragonflies came skimming over the water to peer at the strange traveler, and a turtle on the riverbank stretched out his neck to watch her pass.

Before Alice knew it, the sun had set, and she crouched down to sleep.

Alice was woken the next morning by a great splashing. She had barely opened her eyes when a big fish flew out of the water and disappeared behind a wooden wall.

When Alice saw the fish again, it was in the grip of a hand. The hand lowered the fish to the water, and with a snap of its tail, the fish dove from sight. Alice hoped to stay unseen, but a voice asked,

"What's this?" and she was lifted out of the water, raft and all. Alice found herself looking into the eyes of an old man.

"So, my young friend, where are you off to this fine morning?" he asked.

Alice was afraid. The man was holding a sharp hook tied to a long pole. But she spoke up. She told him she was off to see the sea.

The old man smiled at this. He admired Alice's adventurous spirit, but he knew well that the sea was no place for a little frog on a lily pad. With a twinkle in his eye, he drew a tiny vial from his pocket. "May your journey be safe," he said, handing the bottle to Alice. "But if you should find yourself in trouble, this might be handy."

He said no more but gently set Alice and her raft into the current. Alice called back her thanks to the kindly fisherman. She had no idea what was in the vial or how it could be of help, but she tucked it safely away under her body.

Alice saw many strange and wonderful things that day, including a weathered castle atop a green hill, and a city, with buildings large and small.

As day turned into night, Alice caught a few gnats for dinner and then fell asleep,
dreaming that she was flying with the gulls.

When Alice awoke the next morning, all she could see was blue. She looked in every direction for green riverbanks. In a moment of both joy and fright, she realized that she had reached the sea.

Alice croaked softly. Her voice sounded tiny on the empty water. After a moment, she croaked louder. The only reply was a gust of wind that blew across the surface of the water, making Alice's lily pad twirl in a tight circle. She called out a third time, louder still, and the blue of the sky was slowly overtaken by dark, roiling clouds. The wind began to howl.

Alice was terrified. She thought about swimming for shore but didn't know which way to go. Suddenly a wave rose up, so big that it seemed the sea had grown a mouth. Alice was sure she was going to be swallowed. At the last moment, however, she remembered the fisherman's vial.

As soon as she opened the little bottle, the great wave crashed down, and the patch of sea that carried Alice's raft became absolutely calm. The storm raged on around her, yet she remained dry and safe. By the time the moon hung low in the sky, the wind and waves were gone.

Floating quietly in the middle of nowhere, Alice thought about the many things she had seen beyond the cattails. Yet now she found herself tired, lost, and alone. She longed to be swimming in her pond, diving among the reeds. She began to cry.

"What's the matter?" a soft voice asked. Alice looked around with wide eyes, but saw no one. When the voice asked again, she looked up at the moon.

"I don't belong here," she cried. "I rode the river. I saw the ships and people and cities. I reached the sea, but now I want to go home!"

At that, the moon's reflection on the water seemed to move toward Alice, as if it were a hand reaching out to help. It stopped next to the little frog's lily pad, and the voice whispered, "Come with me. I know the way well."

Alice paddled into the middle of the yellow reflection. She watched and waited, but nothing happened. At last she lowered her eyes—surely she had only imagined the voice. What she saw next, however, made her croak with delight.

She was in the middle of her pond. There were the reeds and the cattails, the treetops just beyond, and the shore barely a dozen kicks away. She dove into the water with a joyful splash and swam all night in the moonlight.

As the spring days grew longer, Alice began to feel restless again. Occasionally birds and animals would visit, but they were always on the move and quickly disappeared. One night she could not sleep, and for the hundredth time since her return, she thought of the moon.

Spring drifted away, and summer arrived. And then, one night, Alice disappeared for the second time.

She was never seen in the little pond again.

Published in 2007 by Creative Editions

P.O. Box 227, Mankato, MN 56002 USA

Creative Editions is an imprint of The Creative Company.

Designed by Rita Marshall. Edited by Aaron Frisch

Printed in Italy

Library of Congress Cataloging-in-Publication Data

Billout, Guy. The frog who wanted to see the sea / by Guy Billout.

Summary: Feeling adventurous one day, a frog leaves her pond
and sets out to visit the great sea she has heard so much about.

ISBN: 978-1-56846-188-5

[1. Frogs—Fiction.] I. Title.

PZ7.B4997Fro 2007   [E]—dc22   2005051898

First Edition

2 4 6 8 9 7 5 3 1